This book belongs to:

_____

What Does the Wind Say?

The illustrations were created using watercolor
The text type was set in New Century Schoolbook
Composed in the United States of America
Designed by Lois A. Rainwater
Edited by Kristen McCurry

Books for Young Readers
11571 K-Tel Drive
Minnetonka, MN 55343
www.tnkidsbooks.com

Library of Congress Cataloging-in-Publication Data

Silvano, Wendi J.
What does the wind say? / by Wendi Silvano ; illustrated by Joan M. Delehanty.

p. cm.

ISBN 1-55971-954-0
1. Nature--Juvenile poetry. 2. Children's poetry, American. I. Delehanty, Joan M., ill. II. Title.

PS3619.I5445W47 2006

811'.6--dc22   2005038019

Printed in Singapore
10 9 8 7 6 5 4 3 2 1

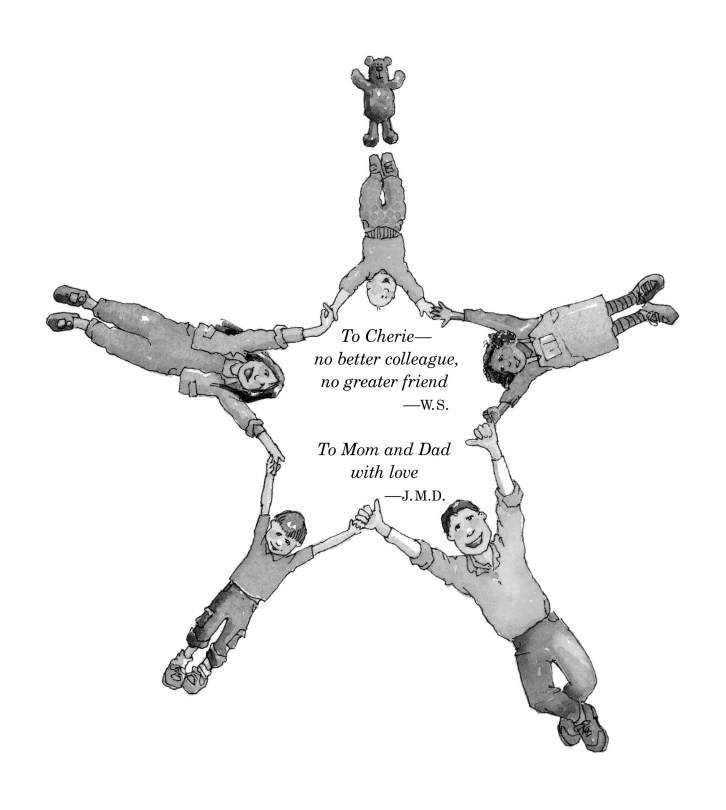

To Cherie—
no better colleague,
no greater friend
—W.S.

To Mom and Dad
with love
—J.M.D.

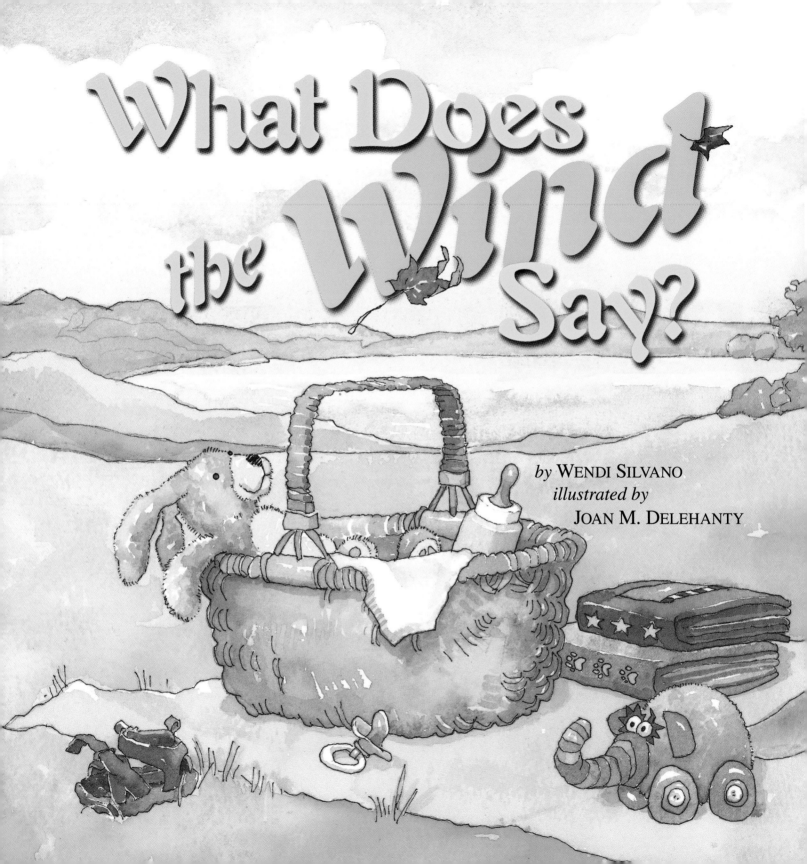

What Does the Wind Say?

by WENDI SILVANO

illustrated by

JOAN M. DELEHANTY

NorthWord
Minnetonka, Minnesota

What does the wind say?

"Whish-
a-
whoo."

What does the moon play?

Peek-a-boo!

What do the stars do?

What does your daddy do?
Kiss good night.

What's in a sunbeam?

Gleam and glow.

What's in a storm cloud?

Crisp,
new
snow.

What's in a dirt patch?

Rocks and bugs.

What's in your mommy's arms?
Squeezy hugs.

What does the rain do?

DriP, driP, droP.

What does a frog do?

Hop, flip, flop.

What does a cat do?

Crawl
and
creep.

What does my baby do?

Sleep, sleep, sleep.

WENDI SILVANO was born in Salt Lake City, Utah, and has lived in Oregon, Peru, and now Colorado. She has a B.A. in Early Childhood Education and taught school for eleven years. She is now an award-winning writer and works from her home, where she gets plenty of "squeezy hugs" from her husband, five kids, two dogs, and a cat.

JOAN M. DELEHANTY graduated with honors from Art Center College of Design in Pasadena, California. She honed her illustration skills designing computer games before launching her own illustration business, Joan of Art, in Seattle. Joan shares her studio with a small crew of four-legged critters who model and provide inspiration for her whimsical watercolors.